Published 1986 by Hamlyn Publishing,
Bridge House, London Road, Twickenham, Middlesex, England

Copyright © Hamlyn Publishing 1986
a division of The Hamlyn Publishing Group Limited.

ISBN 0 600 31135 X
Printed in Italy

·THE CAT·
that Played the Flute

Written and Illustrated by Anne and Ken Mckie

HAMLYN

There was once a cat called Kilkenny. He lived in a little stone cottage with his Master and Mistress, in a place where the mountains reached down to the sea.

Now Kilkenny played the flute. He played so well that everybody from miles around came to listen and dance to his marvellous music.

Kilkenny loved to sit on the rocks near the sea and play his flute really loudly, as the waves crashed on to the shore. One morning he noticed the strangest man dressed all in black.

He was standing on the rocks waving his arms up and down. 'Oh dear!'
thought Kilkenny, 'If he doesn't get off that rock soon he'll be cut off by the tide.'

'Hurry up sir!' yelled the cat, 'Or you'll drown.' The man held on to Kilkenny's flute and scrambled up the rocks to safety.

'You look just like a wet penguin,' giggled Kilkenny.
'I am a GREAT CONDUCTOR,' said the man with a bow.
'Really!' replied the cat looking very interested. 'Is that your bus up there?'

'I'm not a bus conductor,' the man chuckled. 'I am an orchestra conductor! And I have brought all my orchestra on holiday.' Just then a loud trumpeting noise came from inside the bus.

'Are they playing their instruments?' asked Kilkenny. The Great Conductor went rather red.

'No, they're all snoring. I can't find any new tunes for them to play, so they've locked themselves in the bus, and refuse to wake up.'

It just so happens, that the orchestra bus had parked in a field full of animals. And they had all gathered round when they heard the snoring. This gave Kilkenny a great idea.

First he whispered to the donkeys, then to the pigs, then to the goats and the dairy cows. The Great Conductor looked puzzled. 'All together now,' cried Kilkenny. 'One, two, three, . . .'

What a din! It echoed across the fields, three times round the mountains and back again. The orchestra jumped out of their seats and came tumbling out of the bus.

The Great Conductor laughed so much he almost fell into the tuba. 'I'll play you some new tunes on my flute,' said Kilkenny to the orchestra. 'That is, if I can stop laughing.'

So Kilkenny played the best tunes he knew. And when the orchestra heard such lovely music played by a cat on a flute, they felt quite ashamed for sitting snoring in their bus.

Kilkenny's Mistress made some tea, and they all had a picnic on the grass. 'We must start rehearsing straight away,' said the Great Conductor, 'and Kilkenny must play his flute.'

'You can't play dressed like that,' said Kilkenny's Master with a grin. 'Where are your holiday clothes?'

'Whooppee,' yelled the whole orchestra, and they changed into their shorts and tee-shirts. They grabbed their instruments and ran on to the beach. Kilkenny played his flute and the orchestra joined in . . . it sounded beautiful.

They played together on the beach every day for a fortnight. Until at last the Great Conductor told them it was time to go back home. The orchestra felt very sad.

That night the Great Conductor went to Kilkenny's cottage. 'Will you let Kilkenny come back with us and play his flute in a concert?' he begged the cat's Master.

24

So Kilkenny gave his first concert. No one had ever seen a cat that played the flute before. The audience were thrilled. They clapped and cheered and sent him bunches of flowers.

Every day people queued to buy tickets for his concerts. They arrived at the concert hall early in the morning and waited all day. Sometimes the queue

26

stretched twice round the concert hall, right down the street and up the other side. And they all came to hear the cat that played the flute.

Every night Kilkenny would telephone his Master to tell him about the concert.
His Master sounded very sad because he missed his cat so much.
'It's time I went back home,' Kilkenny decided.
'Please play your tunes just once more,' said the Great Conductor, and he
gave the orchestra a big wink.

So Kilkenny was taken into a big empty room. The Great Conductor sat outside and peered at him through a window. 'How strange,' thought Kilkenny. 'Here I am playing to nobody!'

Next day it was time to say goodbye. The Great Conductor smiled at Kilkenny.
'Here is your very own record – you made it yesterday.' And he gave him lots of copies.

Back at home Kilkenny often plays his record and every year the whole
orchestra, the Great Conductor and Kilkenny get together and make beautiful music.